The Magic Button

Written by
Kirsty Holmes

Illustrated by
Brandon Mattless

Chapter One

Jacob's Birthday

Jacob had a good time at his birthday party, but he was secretly glad it was over.

All day, he had been wishing he could just go home. His tummy was full of cake, and Mum had put his presents into the car. But he just wanted to play another level of Eco Warriors before bed.

Eco Warriors was Jacob's favourite video game. He was almost at the end of level six.

In the game, Jacob could be anything he wanted to be, like a brave soldier, or a magical elf. Then Jacob didn't need to feel worried or upset anymore.

04/21 TEN

Books should be returned or renewed by the last
date above. Renew by phone **03000 41 31 31** or
online *www.kent.gov.uk/libs*

Libraries Registration & Archives

Level 10 – White

Helpful Hints for Reading at Home

The focus phonemes (units of sound) used throughout this series are in line with the order in which your child is taught at school. This offers a consistent approach to learning whether reading at home or in the classroom.

HERE ARE SOME COMMON WORDS THAT YOUR CHILD MIGHT FIND TRICKY:

water	where	would	know	thought	through	couldn't
laughed	eyes	once	we're	school	can't	our

TOP TIPS FOR HELPING YOUR CHILD TO READ:

- Encourage your child to read aloud as well as silently to themselves.
- Allow your child time to absorb the text and make comments.
- Ask simple questions about the text to assess understanding.
- Encourage your child to clarify the meaning of new vocabulary.

This book focuses on developing independence, fluency and comprehension. It is a white level 10 book band.

Jacob worried a lot. He was worried this might be a giant storm. There were grey clouds above and big gusts of wind outside.

Jacob was secretly afraid of storms. He didn't want anyone to think he was scared. He just wanted to go home.

"Oh look, Jacob. There's a card for you," said Mum.

"It must be from Auntie Nush," said Dad. "Look at that flower!"

"Typical Auntie Nush! She is always running off somewhere," said Jacob.

Jacob, my darling boy!

Sorry I'm not there today buddy, but I got stuck on a trip to see the rare giant puffball mushroom! This is just so rare that I could not pass it up!

Also, we broke down and it is a long walk back to the car...

Anyhow, it's all utter madness! I do hope you have a fun birthday.

Love and hugs,
Auntie Nush

P.S. When it is a full moon, put the button under the moonlight. Trust me. N xx

Chapter Two

Moonlight and Magic

"Is it a full moon tonight?" asked Dad.
"I think it is," said Mum. "Shall we put the button on your windowsill, Jacob?"

Jacob didn't think anything would happen, but he let Mum put it on the windowsill anyway.

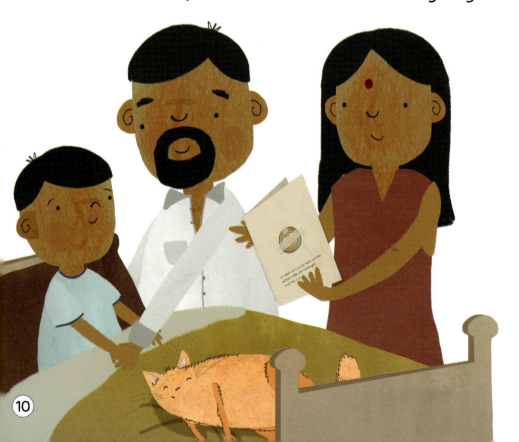

Later on, Jacob was asleep. Mum and Dad were asleep. Even Ginger the cat was asleep. The Moon was full, and it moved slowly across the sky. On the windowsill sat the button.

Jacob was woken up by a long, low hum.
It seemed to be coming from the windowsill!

He got out of bed and tiptoed over to the
window. The hum was coming from the button!

Jacob picked up the button. It felt like it was pulsing in his hand. He slid the window open and held the button out into the moonlight.

For just a moment, it felt like there was magic in the air.

Then the button began to glow!

"Oh Ginger," whispered Jacob. "What is going on?"

Puff! Puff! Puff! Little cubes were popping up all around him!
"It's alright, puss!" cried Jacob, as the little cubes of colour started to rush around. "Jump over here!"

Jacob's bedroom was rushing in towards the TV now, and Jacob was getting sucked in!
"Oh no!" shouted Jacob.
Jacob was sure he could hear the music from Eco Warriors...
What was going on?

Jacob hit the ground with a giant thud. He got up and looked around.

There were grass cubes under his feet. There were cube leaves... on cube trees!
A bunny cube hopped by, carrying a carrot cube.
"Where are we, buddy?" said Jacob to Ginger.

Jacob looked down at his own hands. They were square too!
Jacob looked down at Ginger.
"Ginger! You are completely made of squares. Are they pixels? Can it be?" he said. "Have we been sucked inside my video game?"

Chapter Three

Let's Play

Suddenly, a musical voice behind him called out, making him jump.

"Well, hello my little buddy!"

That kind of voice could only belong to one kind of person.

The kind of person who would send you a magic button for your birthday...

"Auntie Nush! I'm so glad to see you!" cried Jacob. Auntie Nush's flowery armour glinted in the sunshine.

Auntie Nush was a flower expert. Her job took her all over the world looking for flowers. She could grow a flower anywhere, Mum had said. There was one growing out of her helmet right now.

"So, buddy. Are you up for some fun? This game looks great!" said Auntie Nush.

"Are we going to play?" asked Jacob.

"You bet we are!" said Auntie Nush. "Starting with the rest of level six. Let's get stuck in!"

+ 20

+ 10

+ 10

+ 5

AUNTIE NUSH

45

- 5

Suddenly, rubbish started raining down from the sky!

"Auntie Nush! You must sort the rubbish into the right bin!" shouted Jacob.

"Righto, bud! How do I kick?" asked Auntie Nush.

"You're an Eco Warrior now. Try and find your special move," said Jacob. "Here's mine!"

+100

JACOB

100

Push! Kick! Throw! Jacob and Auntie Nush put the rubbish into the correct bins as fast as they could. Still, the rubbish rained down! "Keep going, Jacob! This is fun!" cried Auntie Nush.

At last, all the rubbish had been put into the correct bins.

Suddenly, flowers pushed through the ground and all the animals came out of their hiding places. There were birds and rabbits. There were bulls and chickens. There were bugs and foxes. The level was saved!
"And we got 100 coins!" said Jacob.

LEVEL COMPLETE
100

Level seven was a lot more gloomy than level six. This part of the forest had no sunshine. It was hushed and quiet. Huge chimneys puffed giant clouds of smog into the air.

"Oh, no. The poor forest," said Auntie Nush. A cold wind began to blow.

The big chimneys began to blow low puffs of smog toward Jacob and Auntie Nush.
"Auntie Nush," said Jacob in a low voice.
"It's time for your special move."
Auntie Nush lifted a bunch of flowers. She had a gleam in her eye.
"It's time for some flower power!" she yelled.

Auntie Nush used her flower sword to pummel a cloud of smog. It faded slowly into a grey puff and was gone.

"Good shot, Auntie Nush! Let's show this pollution who's boss!"

Jacob gave a cloud a push with his whip. Auntie Nush gave a great swipe with her sword and took down six at once!

Even Ginger got into the swing of things. She jumped and tumbled. Soon, the smog was gone.

The path was covered in thorny bushes.

"Do you think it's this way, Jacob?" said Auntie Nush slowly.

"Yes, I think it must be," gulped Jacob. "This looks like the boss level to me."

Chapter Four

Into the Storm

Jacob was right. It was the boss level!
"The final push," said Auntie Nush.

The boss they had to fight was... A giant thundercloud!

"Oh no!" gasped Jacob. His knees felt mushy and his heart was beating very quickly. "Anything but that."

"Jacob? Are you OK?" asked Auntie Nush.
"No. I can't do it," said Jacob. He hung his
head. "I'm afraid of storms." He ran to Auntie
Nush for a hug. "I am a wuss!" Jacob said.

Auntie Nush shook her head.
"No, Jacob. You see, it is easy to think you are
brave when there is nothing much to be afraid
of. Real courage comes when you know you are
afraid, but you do what must be done anyway."
Jacob looked up at the thundercloud. He
gripped the button in his hand.

Jacob grabbed his whip. He threw it up and it hung on a rock. Jacob pulled himself up and looked at the thundercloud huffing and puffing below.

He took a big breath, swung across the gap, then jumped - right into the centre of the cloud!

Jacob held out the button between his fingers. It caught a glimmer of light and shone brightly. The light grew brighter and brighter until...
BOOM!

Chapter Five

Hometime for Heroes

The thundercloud had gone, and there was no more thunder and lightning to upset the animals.

"That was unreal!" said Auntie Nush. "I am so utterly proud of you."

Ginger pushed her gently.

"And you, puss cat!"

"Time to go now, Jacob," said Auntie Nush.
"I have things to do in the jungle!"
"Great to see you, Auntie Nush," said Jacob.
"I had a totally amazing time."
They had a big hug.
"Put that button in a safe place," said Auntie
Nush. "See you soon, buddy!"
And then she was gone in a puff of pixels.

In the morning, Jacob's mum and dad came to wake him up.
"What could have happened to Jacob? Why is he all wet?" said Mum.
"Why are his pajamas singed?" said Dad.
"And what happened to Ginger?" they said.

Jacob slept just like a hero.
And he still held the magic button in his hand...

The Magic Button

1. Where did Mum put the button?

   (a)   On the TV

   (b)   On the windowsill

   (c)   On the table

2. What woke Jacob up?

3. How many coins did Jacob and Auntie Nush earn in level six?

4. What was Auntie Nush's special move?

5. Why was Jacob afraid? Have you ever had to have courage?

©2020 **BookLife Publishing Ltd.**
King's Lynn, Norfolk PE30 4LS

ISBN 978–1–83927–020–8

The Magic Button
Written by Kirsty Holmes
Illustrated by Brandon Mattless

An Introduction to BookLife Readers...

Our Readers have been specifically created in line with the London Institute of Education's approach to book banding and are phonetically decodable and ordered to support each phase of the Letters and Sounds document.

Each book has been created to provide the best possible reading and learning experience. Our aim is to share our love of books with children, providing both emerging readers and prolific page–turners with beautiful books that are guaranteed to provoke interest and learning, regardless of ability.

BOOK BAND GRADED using the Institute of Education's approach to levelling.

PHONETICALLY DECODABLE supporting each phase of Letters and Sounds.

EXERCISES AND QUESTIONS to offer reinforcement and to ascertain comprehension.

BEAUTIFULLY ILLUSTRATED to inspire and provoke engagement, providing a variety of styles for the reader to enjoy whilst reading through the series.

AUTHOR INSIGHT:
KIRSTY HOLMES

Kirsty Holmes, holder of a BA, PGCE, and an MA, was born in Norfolk, England. She has written over 60 books for BookLife Publishing, and her stories are full of imagination, creativity and fun.

This book focuses on developing independence, fluency and comprehension. It is a white level 10 book band.

The Magic Pea

Written by
Madeline Tyler

Illustrated by
Margherita Borin

Anya's mum was a vet in a town far away.
Anya dreamed of being a vet one day, just like
her mum.